Published by
North Atlantic Books
Berkeley, California

Cover design by Jasmine Hromjak
Printed in China

Dino Does Yoga is sponsored and published by the Society for the Study of Native Arts and Sciences (dba North Atlantic Books), an educational nonprofit based in Berkeley, California, that collaborates with partners to develop cross-cultural perspectives, nurture holistic views of art, science, the humanities, and healing, and seed personal and global transformation by publishing work on the relationship of body, spirit, and nature.

North Atlantic Books' publications are available through most bookstores. For further information, visit our website at www.northatlanticbooks.com or call 800-733-3000.

Library of Congress Cataloging-in-Publication Data
Names: Engström von Alten, Sofie, author.
Title: Dino does yoga / Sofie Engström von Alten.
Description: Berkeley, California : North Atlantic Books, 2019. | Summary: As a newly-hatched tyrannosaurus rex discovers the world around him, he imitates everything from a dragonfly to a mountain by doing a fifteen-pose yoga sequence.
Identifiers: LCCN 2018056271 (print) | LCCN 2018059508 (ebook) | ISBN 9781623173074 (ebook) | ISBN 9781623173067 (hardback)
Subjects: | CYAC: Stories in rhyme. | Yoga—Fiction. | Tyrannosaurus rex—Fiction. | Dinosaurs--Fiction. | Animals—Infancy—Fiction. | BISAC: JUVENILE FICTION / Animals / Dinosaurs & Prehistoric Creatures. | JUVENILE FICTION / Sports & Recreation / General. | JUVENILE FICTION / Health & Daily Living / General.
Classification: LCC PZ8.3.E584 (ebook) | LCC PZ8.3.E584 Din 2019 (print) | DDC [E]—dc23
LC record available at https://lccn.loc.gov/2018056271

Printed and bound by Qualibre (NJ)/PrintPlus, February 2019, in Hong Kong, Job #S190200016

1 2 3 4 5 6 7 8 9 10 Qualibre/PrintPlus 25 24 23 22 21 20 19

North Atlantic Books is committed to the protection of our environment. We partner with FSC-certified printers using soy-based inks and print on recycled paper whenever possible.

DINO DOES YOGA

Sofie Engström von Alten

North Atlantic Books
Berkeley, California

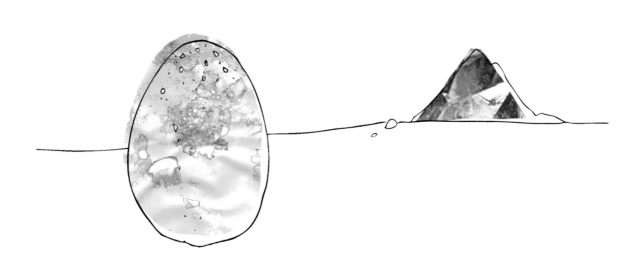

Long ago and far away
a lonely egg has lost its way.

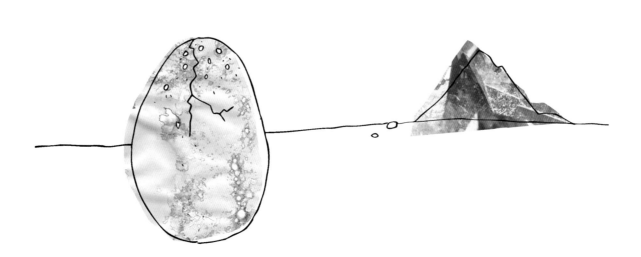

Day by day, ever so slow
a tiny crack begins to show.

The first thing to catch Dino's eye
is a giant buzzing dragonfly.

DRAGONFLY POSE

Dino wants to fly as well,
freshly popped out of his shell.
Back is straight, feet together,
flapping legs light as a feather!

Look! A mountain far away.
Dino stands up, straightaway.

Feet apart and open hands,
Dino is as strong as this new land!

MOUNTAIN
POSE

SNIFF!

Deep breath in, arms up high,
Dino tries to touch the sky!

MOUNTAIN
POSE

One small step for Dino's kind,
arms reach up with hips aligned!

WARRIOR
ONE POSE

Reaching arms out far and wide—
a Pterodactyl is our guide.

WARRIOR
TWO POSE

Dino lifts his left leg high
with steady tail and focused eyes.

WARRIOR
THREE POSE

What is this shining thing?
How flowing, cool,
and beckoning!

Dino wants to look up close
and maybe touch it with his nose.
Reaching for those pointy toes
let's see how this water flows.

FORWARD
BEND

Dino dips his little muzzle
deep into the shining puddle.
So delicious, fresh, and sweet,
bending down toward our feet!

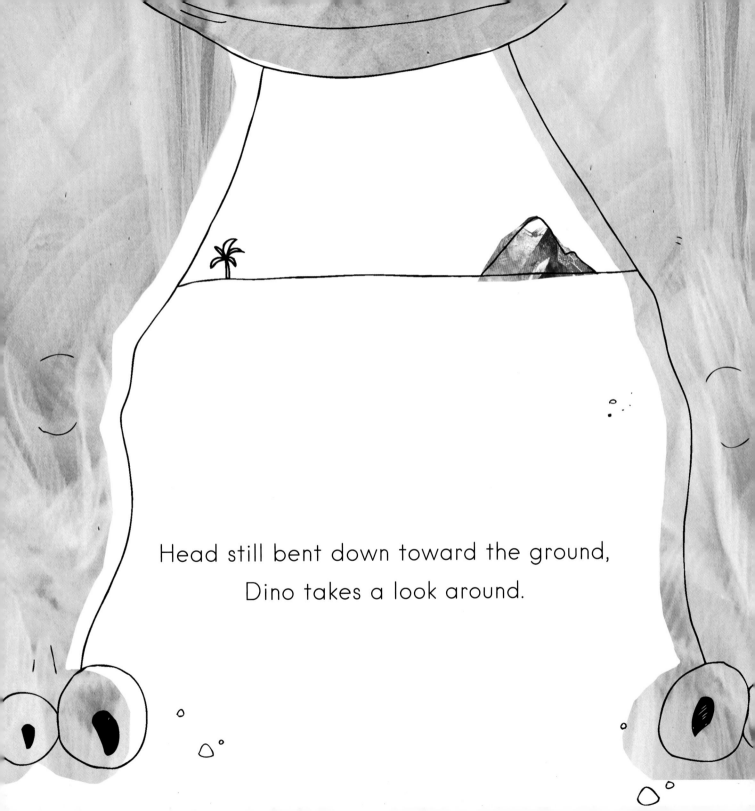

Head still bent down toward the ground,
Dino takes a look around.

DOWNWARD DINO POSE

Exhaling—ahh! One breath more
reaching for the sandy floor.

What's crawling there, between those feet?
Maybe something nice to eat!
Bending more, he sees a bunch—
those ants could be a yummy lunch!

Legs are planted nice and wide.
A tasty snack cannot hide!

WIDE-LEGGED
BEND

Dino loves to munch on ants,
but this requires a steady stance.
Deltoids in, belly strong,
Dino's spine is straight and long.

PLANK
POSE

Now all the ants have gone away,
and Dino's hunger is at bay!
He lifts his head above his shoulders—
abdominals in, tight as boulders.

COBRA
POSE

What's that swaying in the sky?
It's a palm tree, way up high!

How strong and tall
this tree is standing
and every day it is expanding.
Coming onto two strong feet,
Dino attempts this mighty feat.
Raising arms to highest height,
he reaches up with all his might.
Then the hardest part of all—
raise one leg, try not to fall!

TREE POSE

THUMP!

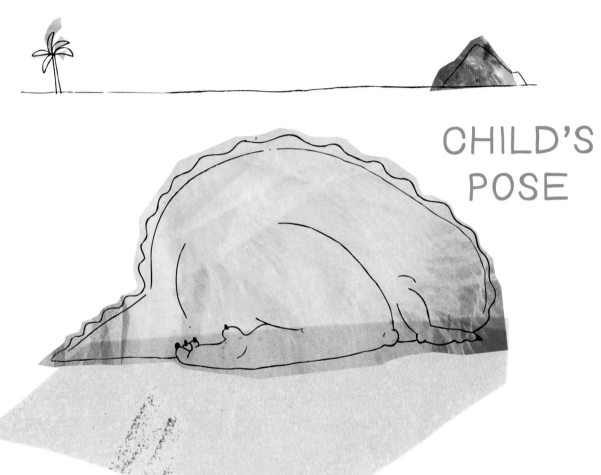

CHILD'S
POSE

It's okay, little Dino!
Everyone falls down sometimes
and even wrong words seem to rhyme.

Let's readjust...

EASY POSE

Legs in the lead.

Those pointy claws are sharp indeed!

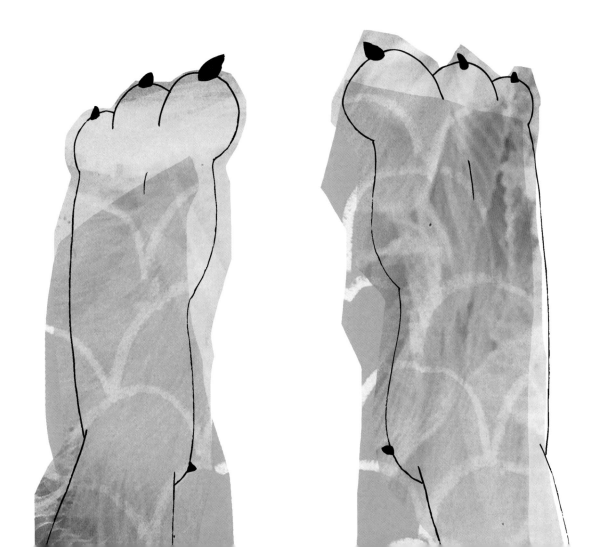

FORWARD FOLD

Leaning forward, Dino's reach
aims for his toes, hamstrings release.

Phew! Yoga sure makes Dino tired.

So much energy is required!

But now the time has come to rest.

He lies on his back, inflated chest.

Muscles relaxed, nothing stressed...

Let's let gravity do the rest.

RELAXATION
POSE

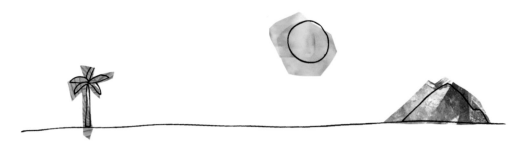

SOFIE ENGSTRÖM VON ALTEN is an illustrator and yoga instructor. Born and raised on the beautiful West Coast in San Francisco, California, Sofie grew up bilingual. Exploring the world through art, yoga, and travel has always held her greatest fascination. After visiting more than fifty countries, Sofie studied yoga nestled in the Indian Himalayas with the masters. Upon returning to the West, she found yoga to be a wonderful tool for teaching kids—both in the classroom and under a tree. Sofie continues to create hyperkitsch illustrations and teach yoga to children and adults.

www.hyperkitsch.com

About North Atlantic Books

North Atlantic Books (NAB) is an independent, nonprofit publisher committed to a bold exploration of the relationships between mind, body, spirit, and nature. Founded in 1974, NAB aims to nurture a holistic view of the arts, sciences, humanities, and healing. To make a donation or to learn more about our books, authors, events, and newsletter, please visit www.northatlanticbooks.com.

North Atlantic Books is the publishing arm of the Society for the Study of Native Arts and Sciences, a 501(c)(3) nonprofit educational organization that promotes cross-cultural perspectives linking scientific, social, and artistic fields. To learn how you can support us, please visit our website.